A Note to Parents and Caregivers:

Read-it! Readers are for children who are just starting on the amazing road to reading. These beautiful books support both the acquisition of reading skills and the love of books.

 The PURPLE LEVEL presents basic topics and objects using high frequency words and simple language patterns.

 The RED LEVEL presents familiar topics using common words and repeating sentence patterns.

 The BLUE LEVEL presents new ideas using a larger vocabulary and varied sentence structure.

 The YELLOW LEVEL presents more challenging ideas, a broad vocabulary, and wide variety in sentence structure.

 The GREEN LEVEL presents more complex ideas, an extended vocabulary range, and expanded language structures.

 The ORANGE LEVEL presents a wide range of ideas and concepts using challenging vocabulary and complex language structures.

When sharing a book with your child, read in short stretches, pausing often to talk about the pictures. Have your child turn the pages and point to the pictures and familiar words. And be sure to reread favorite stories or parts of stories.

There is no right or wrong way to share books with children. Find time to read with your child, and pass on the legacy of literacy.

Adria F. Klein, Ph.D.
Professor Emeritus
California State University
San Bernardino, California

For Tootie, my mom (and Tuckerbean's grandma), with love—J.K.

Editor: Christianne Jones
Designer: Amy Bailey Muehlenhardt
Page Production: Tracy Kaehler
Creative Director: Keith Griffin
Editorial Director: Carol Jones
The illustrations in this book were created in watercolor and pen.

Picture Window Books
5115 Excelsior Boulevard
Suite 232
Minneapolis, MN 55416
877-845-8392
www.picturewindowbooks.com

Printed in the United States of America.

Library of Congress Cataloging-in-Publication Data
Kalz, Jill.
Tuckerbean / by Jill Kalz ; illustrated by Benton Mahan.
p. cm. — (Read-it! readers)
Summary: Portrays the amazing adventures a puppy might have while his owner is
away at school.
ISBN 1-4048-1591-0 (hardcover)
[1. Dogs—Fiction. 2. Animals—Infancy—Fiction. 3. Imagination—Fiction.]
I. Mahan, Benton, ill. II. Title. III. Series.

PZ7.K12655Tuc 2005
[E]—dc22   2005021458

Tuckerbean

by Jill Kalz
illustrated by Benton Mahan

Special thanks to our advisers for their expertise:

Adria F. Klein, Ph.D.
Professor Emeritus, California State University
San Bernardino, California

Susan Kesselring, M.A.
Literacy Educator
Rosemount–Apple Valley–Eagan (Minnesota) School District

PiCTURE WiNDOW BOOKS
Minneapolis, Minnesota

Before I go to school each day,
I say goodbye to Tuckerbean.

5

He sniffles and snuffles. His tongue
rolls out. His shiny black eyes blink
in time with the clock.

But when the bus turns the corner,
I think he smiles real wide. His tail
thumps like a drum. Adventures fill
his puppy head.

Tuckerbean hops on a racehorse.

They thunder down the track.

Tuckerbean climbs the stairs of the tallest lighthouse.

He saves a ship from the rocks.

Tuckerbean rides in a hot-air balloon.

Seeing peach trees makes him drool.

Tuckerbean wears beads, feathers, and a mask.

He throws confetti in the air.

When the clock strikes three, I come home from school. Tuckerbean yawns. He scratches. He stretches.

19

"Did you have good dreams? Did you chase bunnies? Did you bury a bone?" I ask Tuckerbean.

20

Tuckerbean winks, jumps up, and
licks my face.

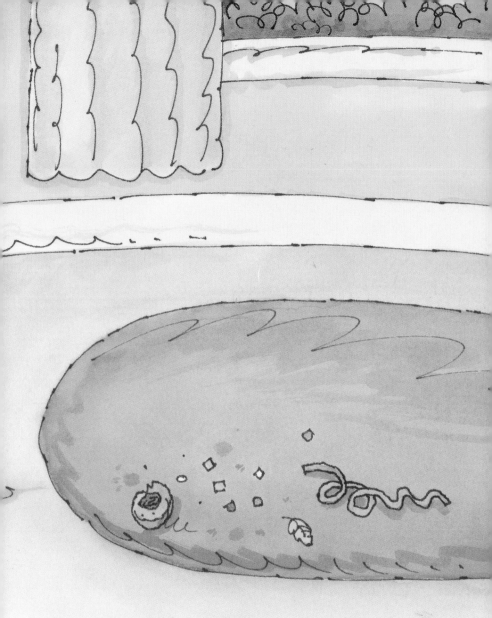

I think my little dog has a
big secret!

More *Read-it!* Readers

Bright pictures and fun stories help you practice your reading skills. Look for more books at your level.

At the Beach 1-4048-0651-2
Bears on Ice 1-4048-1577-5
The Bossy Rooster 1-4048-0051-4
Dust Bunnies 1-4048-1168-0
Flying with Oliver 1-4048-1583-X
Frog Pajama Party 1-4048-1170-2
Jack's Party 1-4048-0060-3
The Lifeguard 1-4048-1584-8
The Playground Snake 1-4048-0556-7
Recycled! 1-4048-0068-9
Robin's New Glasses 1-4048-1587-2
The Sassy Monkey 1-4048-0058-1
What's Bugging Pamela? 1-4048-1189-3

Looking for a specific title or level? A complete list of *Read-it!* Readers is available on our Web site:
www.picturewindowbooks.com